Concord Theatricals Acting Edition

The Lightning Thief

Theatre for Young Audiences Edition

Book by Joe Tracz

Music & Lyrics by
Rob Rokicki

Adapted from the book
The Lightning Thief by
Rick Riordan

concord
theatricals

ISBN 978-0573-70951-7

www.concordtheatricals.com
www.concordtheatricals.co.uk

No one shall make any changes in this title(s) for the purpose of production. No part of this book may be reproduced, stored in a retrieval system, scanned, uploaded, or transmitted in any form, by any means, now known or yet to be invented, including mechanical, electronic, digital, photocopying, recording, videotaping, or otherwise, without the prior written permission of the publisher. No one shall share this title(s), or any part of this title(s), through any social media or file hosting websites.

For all inquiries regarding motion picture, television, online/digital and other media rights, please contact Concord Theatricals Corp.

THIRD-PARTY MATERIALS USE NOTE

Licensees are solely responsible for obtaining formal written permission from copyright owners to use copyrighted third-party materials (e.g., incidental music not provided in connection with a performance license, artworks, logos) in the performance of this play and are strongly cautioned to do so. If no such permission is obtained by the licensee, then the licensee must use only original materials and materials that the licensee owns and controls. Licensees are solely responsible and liable for clearances of all third-party copyrighted materials, and shall indemnify the copyright owners of the play(s) and their licensing agent, Concord Theatricals Corp., against any costs, expenses, losses and liabilities arising from the use of such copyrighted third-party materials by licensees. For music, please contact the appropriate music licensing authority in your territory for the rights to any incidental music not provided in connection with a performance license.

IMPORTANT BILLING AND CREDIT REQUIREMENTS

If you have obtained performance rights to this title, please refer to your licensing agreement for important billing and credit requirements.

THE LIGHTNING THIEF debuted in 2014 as a one-hour musical at the Lucille Lortel Theatre off-Broadway. After a national tour, an expanded version of the show returned to the Lucille Lortel Theatre in 2017. The show toured again, and on October 16, 2019, *The Lightning Thief* opened on Broadway at the Longacre Theatre. The original Broadway production was produced by TheaterWorksUSA, Martian Entertainment, Victoria Lang, Lisa Chanel, Jennifer Doyle & Roy Lennox, Meredith Lucio,Van Dean, O'Hara, Rae, Zurcher, Wei-Hwa Huang, Stewart F. Lane, Bonnie Comley, Leah Lane, Tosha Martin, Cara Talty, Fisher, Jacobs Baker, Masotti, Prince, Schroeder Shapiro Productions, Retsios Boghosian, and SJGH Productions. The performance was directed by Stephen Brackett, with choreography by Patrick McCollum, Music Supervisor/Musical Director of Orchestrations Wiley DeWeese, scenic design by Lee Savage, costume design by Sydney Maresca, lighting design by David Lander, sound design by Ryan Rumery and Production Manager Brian Lynch. The cast was as follows:

PERCY JACKSON . . . . Chris McCarrell

ANNABETH . . . . Kristin Stokes

GROVER / MR. D . . . . Jorrel Javier

LUKE & OTHERS . . . . James Hayden Rodriguez

SALLY JACKSON & OTHERS . . . . Jalynn Steele

MR. BRUNNER AKA CHIRON & OTHERS . . . . Ryan Knowles

CLARISSE & OTHERS . . . . Sarah Beth Pfiefer

UNDERSTUDIES / SWINGS . . . . Izzy Figuero, Sam Leicht,
T. Shyvonne Stewart

CHARACTERS

PERCY JACKSON – son of Poseidon, a good kid with a teenage temper.

ANNABETH – daughter of Athena, smarter than you.

GROVER – a happy-go-lucky satyr, like a hippie kid with hooves.

   *MR. D – aka Dionysus, god of wine, snarky camp director.

LUKE – son of Hermes, cool camp counselor.

   *GABE UGLIANO – Percy's foul stepfather.

   *ARES – god of war, rock star in leather pants.

   *MINOTAUR – half-man half-bull.

   *CHARON – ferryman to the Underworld.

SALLY JACKSON – Percy's hard-working mother.

   *MRS. DODDS – a Fury posing as a substitute algebra teacher.

   *CLARISSE – tough jock girl, daughter of Ares.

   *THE ORACLE – a hippie mummy.

   *AUNTY EM – aka Medusa, avid sculptor.

   *THALIA – daughter of Zeus, brave.

   *BIANCA – a mysterious girl in 1930's clothes.

   *CHIMERA

MR. BRUNNER – aka **CHIRON** – wise centaur, part-time Latin teacher.

   *POSEIDON – god of the sea, salty beach bum.

   *HADES – god of the dead, aging rock-star type.

   *KRONOS – a voice in a pit.

   *CYCLOPS

   *BUS DRIVER

   *UBER DRIVER

*Characters with an asterisk are played by the primary cast: Percy, Annabeth, Grover, Luke, Sally Jackson, and Mr Brunner. Doubling is not required but this cast breakdown can be used as a cast for doubling.

SETTING

Camp Half-Blood, Long Island, NY;
New York; Los Angeles; and places in between.

TIME

Present Day.

AUTHORS' NOTE

For productions where cast size isn't a concern, we encourage you to cast as many actors as you wish, and experiment with doubling based on your own needs. We also encourage you to look beyond traditional casting "types" when it comes to the characters' race, gender, and physical ability. Above all, the characters in *The Lightning Thief* are gods and heroes – and gods and heroes can look like any of us.

Our production used imaginative, suggestive props and costuming to bring Percy's world to life. Part of the joy of Rick Riordan's books is the way they mash together Greek mythology and modern sensibilities in fun and surprising ways – for example, Poseidon, the sea-god, doesn't wear a toga but a Hawaiian shirt. We let that mash-up spirit guide our vision, finding creative, minimalist solutions to the challenge of staging a big, fantastical world. In your own production, we encourage you to rely on theatricality and imagination whenever possible, taking cues from the show's irreverent, rock-and-roll, DIY tone.

MUSICAL NUMBERS

Music 01: "Prologue/The Day I Got Expelled"... Percy, Company

Music 02: "Strong"................................. Sally, Percy

Music 03: "The Minotaur!/The Weirdest".......Percy, Company

Music 04: "Another Terrible Day" .... Mr. D

Music 04A: "She Fought Bravely"

Music 05: "Their Sign" .... Chiron, Percy, Luke

Music 06: "Put You In Your Place".......... Clarisse, Annabeth, Company

Music 06A: "Clarisse Makes A Splash"

Music 06B: "The Trident Appears/Thunder"

Music 07: "The Oracle"................. The Oracle, Company

Music 08: "Good Kid" ....Percy, Company

Music 09: "Killer Quest!" .... Percy, Grover, Annabeth, Company

Music 10: "The Tree On The Hill" .... Grover, Luke, Annabeth, Thalia

Music 10A: "A Visit With Aunty Em"

Music 11: "My Grand Plan"......................... Annabeth

Music 12: "Drive"...... Grover, Percy, Annabeth, Ares, Ensemble

Music 13: "The Weirdest Dream (Reprise)"................ Percy

Music 13A: "Hellevator"

Music 13B: "It's The Pits"

Music 13C: "Hello Hades"

Music 13D: "Sally Appears"

Music 14A: "Poseidon Finally Shows Up"

Music 14B: "Reunited"

Music 15: "The Last Day Of Summer" ..... Percy, Luke, Company

Music 16: "Bring On The Monsters"...................Company

Music 16A: "Bows/Exit Music"

(Sound Effects: Thunder! The Half-Bloods enter: **LUKE, ANNABETH, GROVER,** *and* **CLARISSE.***)*

[MUSIC NO 01 – PROLOGUE/THE DAY I GOT EXPELLED]

LUKE.
> THE GODS ARE REAL.
> LIKE THE GREEK GODS.

ANNABETH.
> LIKE THE ONES YOU LEARNED ABOUT
> BUT WEREN'T PAYING ATTENTION TO.

GROVER.
> WELL, THEY DON'T PAY ATTENTION TO YOU, EITHER.

CLARISSE.
> ESPECIALLY IF YOU'RE THEIR KID.

ALL HALF-BLOODS.
> YEAH, THE GODS ARE REAL.
> AND THEY HAVE KIDS.
> AND THOSE KIDS HAVE ISSUES!
> ISSUES!

LUKE & GROVER.
> DADDY DOESN'T LOVE ME
> AND MOMMY IS A GOD.

ANNABETH & CLARISSE.
> MOMMY CAN'T PROTECT ME
> AND DADDY IS A GOD.

ALL HALF-BLOODS.

>MOMMY IS TOO BUSY
>AND DADDY IS TOO BUSY.
>BUSY, BUSY, BUSY, BUSY
>BEING A GOD, YEAH!
>YOU NEVER LISTEN TO ME
>YOU NEVER LISTEN.
>YOU NEVER LISTEN
>BUT NOW YOU'RE GONNA LISTEN,
>'CAUSE IT'S TIME YOU HEARD OUR SIDE OF THE STORY.
>IT'S TIME YOU HEARD OUR STORY.

>>(**PERCY JACKSON** *enters.*)

PERCY.

>LOOK.
>I DIDN'T WANT TO BE A HALF-BLOOD.
>I DIDN'T ASK TO BE A HERO, SEEKING PRAISE.
>BEING A HALF-BLOOD IS SCARY,
>IT MOSTLY GETS YOU KILLED IN VERY NASTY WAYS.

>I DIDN'T WANT TO CAUSE TROUBLE, TROUBLE,
>I'M LESS A PLAYER AND MORE THE PLAYED
>AND HONESTLY, I'D TOTALLY BE FINE,
>IF I COULD MAKE IT TO THE NEXT GRADE,
>NEXT GRADE.

>WASN'T THE NASTY BREATH OF MY STEPDAD,
>IT WAS DANGER THAT I SMELLED,
>THE DAY IT ALL WENT DOWN.
>THE DAY I GOT EXPELLED!

Maybe you don't know what a half-blood is, because your life is normal and happy and not constantly in danger. But my life…?

>>(*The* **CHORUS** *creates the tableau of a class field trip at a history museum.*)

Let me set the scene:
>WE WERE ON THIS FREAKY FIELD TRIP.

CHORUS.
FREAKY TRIP...

PERCY.
THAT'S WHEN THIS STORY SHOULD PROBABLY START,

CHORUS.
OOH

ALL.
WE WERE GEEKING OUT ON ANCIENT GREEK,
AT THE NEW YORK METROPOLITAN MUSEUM OF ART!

PERCY.	**CHORUS, GROVER, & MR. BRUNNER.**
WE STOPPED BY ALL THE	STATUES
AND LEARNED ABOUT THE	GODS,

PERCY.
FROM MR. BRUNNER
AND MY SUBSTITUTE, MRS. DODDS,

PERCY.	**CHORUS, GROVER, & MR. BRUNNER.**
HADN'T DONE, NOTHIN' WRONG,	OOH, OOH AHH!
WASN'T RUDE, HADN'T REBELLED!	ON THE DAY IT ALL WENT DOWN
ON THE DAY IT ALL WENT DOWN:	
THE DAY I GOT EXPELLED!	

> (**MR. BRUNNER**, *a distinguished Latin teacher
> in a wheelchair, lectures.* **MRS. DODDS**, *the weird
> substitute, lurks like a vulture by his side.*)

MR. BRUNNER. The Greek Gods! Almighty titans of earth,
sea, and sky! But even they were children once. And
they didn't have it easy! Their father, Kronos feared the
day his children would inherit the earth. So what did
he do? Anyone? Anyone?

MRS. DODDS. *(Gleefully.)* He ate them!

MR. BRUNNER. Ah… thank you, Mrs. Dodds. But! One child, Zeus, escaped, and devised a plan to rescue his brothers and sisters! He tricked Kronos into eating a rock. And what did Kronos do? Anyone? Any *student?*

MRS DODDS. He vomited them up!

PERCY.
WHAA?!
I DIDN'T REALLY GET THE STORY.
AT LEAST IT WASN'T BORING, AS I'D FEARED.
BUT IS IT ME, OR IS GREEK MYTHOLOGY
NOT DEEPLY WEIRD?

> (**GROVER** *lets out a goat bleat that he covers with a cough.* **PERCY** *throws him a strange look.)*

Dude, why do you have peanut butter in your hair?

GROVER. Ask Nancy Bobofit.

PERCY. She threw a peanut butter sandwich at you?

GROVER. She threw a peanut butter sandwich at YOU. I stopped it. With my head.

PERCY. Grover, you're a good friend.

GROVER.
DUDE. I'M YOUR ONLY FRIEND.

MRS. DODDS.
PERCY JACKSON!!!

> (**GROVER** *gives* **PERCY** *a sympathetic look as* **MRS. DODDS** *leads him away.)*

PERCY. Look… if this is about Nancy Bobofit, she only hates me because I stopped her from setting fire to those first graders –

MRS. DODDS. I have heard much about you... *Percy Jackson*. Kicked out of five schools in six years. One might question your parentage.

PERCY. Hey, don't talk about my mom –

MRS. DODDS. And your father? That's right... you don't know who he is.

> (**MRS. DODDS** *lurches towards him, as a pair of bat wings emerge from her back.*)

PERCY. Uh, Mrs. Dodds? You have something growing on your...

CHORUS & PERCY. AAH!

> (**MRS. DODDS** *shrieks and dives at* **PERCY**. *Sound effects: Whoosh!* **MR. BRUNNER** *appears and tosses* **PERCY** *a pen.*)

MR. BRUNNER. What ho, Percy!

PERCY. Mr. Brunner? What am I supposed to do with a pen –

> (**PERCY** *clicks the pen, and suddenly it expands into a sword.*)

Sword! Whoa!

> (*He blocks with the sword. It strikes* **MRS. DODDS**, *who shrieks and dissolves.*)

... Mr. Brunner? ... Mrs. Dodds?

> (*But they both have vanished, and the sword in his hand is now a pen again.*)

UM...

I DIDN'T KNOW WHAT JUST HAD HAPPENED
WAS THAT ALL A CREEPY CRAZY DREAM?
MY TEACHER WAS A CREATURE,
THEN SHE VANISHED IN THE ETHER

WITH A DEMON SCREAM.
THE NEXT THING THAT I KNEW,
I WAS WHERE DETENTION WAS HELD,
THE DAY IT ALL GOT REAL.
THE DAY I GOT –

(**PERCY** *is with* **GROVER** *and* **MR. BRUNNER**.)

Expelled?!?

MR. BRUNNER. I tried, Percy, but the headmaster stands firm in his decision.

PERCY. But it wasn't my fault, it was Mrs. Dodds! She attacked me, and... *you* saw it!

(**MR. BRUNNER** *and* **GROVER** *exchange a look.*)

MR. BRUNNER. Did I?

PERCY. You gave me that pen! Only it wasn't a pen, it was a sword, and... what?

GROVER. Percy... we've never had a teacher named Mrs. Dodds.

MR. BRUNNER. Perhaps it's for the best. This wasn't the place for you. It was only a matter of time before –

PERCY. I got kicked out?

MR. BRUNNER. That's not what I ...

PERCY. You think I'm trouble. Just like everyone else.

MR. BRUNNER. No, but... that is to say... I can only accept the best from you, Percy. Someday you'll understand why. I'm truly sorry.

(**MR. BRUNNER** *exits with* **GROVER**. **PERCY** *slumps.*)

PERCY. Yeah well, I'm sorry I let you down...

PERCY.

SO IF YOU THINK YOU ARE A HALF-BLOOD,
BETTER GET HEADIN' TO THE EXITS NOW.
'CAUSE FOLKS WILL THINK YOU'RE LYIN',
BETTER RUN AND DON'T START CRYIN'
'CAUSE YOU'RE MONSTER CHOW

OR STICK AROUND
AND MAYBE YOU'LL LEARN FROM ME.
THIS AIN'T ODYSSEUS'S ODYSSEY,

PERCY.	**CHORUS, GROVER, & MR. BRUNNER**
SO HEAR ME OUT,	OOH,
IF YOU'RE SO COMPELLED.	OOH AHH
BUT, NOBODY LISTENS TO ME,	OOH
THEY NEVER LISTEN.	
NOBODY LISTENS TO ME!	OOH
THEY NEVER LISTEN, OH.	
	DUDE! YOU GOT EXPELLED!
I DIDN'T WANT TO BE A HALF-BLOOD.	
I DIDN'T ASK TO BE A HALF-BLOOD	EXPELLED!
	CHORUS
EXPELLED!	EXPELLED!

*(***PERCY***'s mom,* **SALLY JACKSON** *appears.)*

I tried to stay out of trouble, Mom. I swear.

SALLY. I don't understand, Percy, what happened on this field trip? *(Off* **PERCY***'s look, she softens.)* You know what, it doesn't matter. We'll find another school. Again.

PERCY. I'm not a bad kid on purpose.

SALLY. Oh, baby, I know. *(Beat, then.)* How would you like to take a trip? Just the two of us.

PERCY. Is that okay with "Smelly Gabe?"

SALLY. I'll deal with your stepfather.

*(**PERCY***'s stepdad,* **GABE UGLIANO,** *enters.)*

GABE. Sally! Where's my bean dip?

SALLY. Gabe, there you are... *(This is hard to say.)* ...dear. How would you like a weekend without Percy and I in your way?

GABE. Who's gonna cook for me? Who's gonna clean?

SALLY. I'll give you a back rub (**GABE***'s still not sold.)* A ... *(This is gonna be gross.)* foot rub?

GABE. *(Giving in.)* Both feet. *(Then, as he exits.)* Bean. Dip.

(He's gone. **SALLY** *exhales.)*

PERCY. Mom... you don't have to put up with him like that.

SALLY. It's complicated, Percy.

PERCY. You always say that. Why?

SALLY. Because the truth might mean saying goodbye to you. For good.

[MUSIC NO. 02 – STRONG]

SALLY. But maybe it's time.

I CAN'T TELL YOU ALL MY SECRETS...

PERCY.

MAYBE YOU SHOULD START WITH ONE:

SALLY.

YOU'RE RIGHT.
I'LL SHOW YOU WHERE I MET YOUR DAD,
HE'D BE PROUD OF HIS SON.

PERCY.
WHO CARES?
WE'RE BETTER OFF WITHOUT HIM.

SALLY.
NO!
IT'S TIME YOU FOUND OUT MORE ABOUT HIM.

> *(They move to the beach. Sound effects: Ocean waves.)*

PERCY. Look at the size of those waves!

SALLY. Fire's going. Someone needs a marshmallow. *(Playful.)* They're blue.

PERCY. You met Dad on this beach?

SALLY.
I FIRST SAW HIM IN THE WATER,
COMING OUT OF THE MORNING MIST.
HE WAS HANDSOME, STRONG, AND BEFORE TOO LONG
YOU CAME TO EXIST.

PERCY.
AND HE DITCHED US.
NO COMING HOME FOR DINNER,
YEAH, HE SOUNDS LIKE A REAL WINNER...

SALLY. He wanted to meet you. And he warned me things might be hard if you were... like him.

PERCY. Was he a screw up too? I'm sorry, Mom, if I was only normal –

SALLY. Hey!
NORMAL IS A MYTH,
EV'RYONE HAS ISSUES THEY'RE DEALING WITH.

PERCY.
MOM –
IF YOU'RE WEIRD, YOU'RE WEAK.

SALLY.
THAT'S WHERE YOU'RE WRONG:
THE THINGS THAT MAKE YOU DIFF'RENT
ARE THE VERY THINGS THAT MAKE YOU
STRONG.
SO BE STRONG.

You'll see. You're destined for great things.

PERCY. The only thing I seemed destined for is detention.
I CAN'T FOCUS.
I SUCK AT SCHOOL.
MY A.D.D. GETS THE BEST OF ME.
DYSLEXIA? NOT COOL.

SALLY.
JUST HANG ON, SON, ONE DAY YOU'LL FIND
YOU'LL LEAVE THAT BORING LITTLE LIFE BEHIND.

SALLY & PERCY.
NORMAL IS A MYTH,
EV'RYONE HAS ISSUES THEY'RE DEALING WITH.

SALLY.
AND THERE'S A PLACE YOU NEED TO GO
WHERE YOU'LL BELONG,
WHERE THE THINGS THAT MAKE YOU DIFF'RENT
ARE THE THINGS THAT MAKE YOU SPECIAL,
SPECIAL LIKE YOUR FATHER,
YES, PERCY, YOU ARE SPECIAL.

(Beat.)

LIKE FOOD THE COLOR BLUE,
ALL THE THINGS THAT MAKE YOU, YOU
ARE THE THINGS THAT WILL MAKE YOU
STRONG.

SALLY & PERCY.
SO BE STRONG.

PERCY. So what is this place? Are you sending me to summer school?

SALLY. More like summer camp. But not any ordinary summer camp. Percy, your father is...

(*Sound effects: Twig snap.* **GROVER** *appears, rear-first: we can't see his face.*)

GROVER. Baaaaah!

PERCY. Oh look, a goat. Hey little guy –

(**GROVER** *stands up and turns around.*)

GROVER. Paaaa-ercy!

[MUSIC NO 03 – THE MINOTAUR!/ THE WEIRDEST DREAM]

PERCY. AAAH! Grover? What are you doing here? ... and what happened to your legs?

GROVER. I've been searching everywhere for you guys.

SALLY. What is it? What's wrong?

GROVER. (*To* **PERCY.**) You didn't tell her about the field trip?

SALLY. (*To* **PERCY.**) What happened on the field trip?

PERCY. (*To* **SALLY.**) You said it didn't matter!

GROVER. (*To* **SALLY.**) He met a Fury.

PERCY. (*To* **GROVER.**) YOU'RE all furry! What happened to your legs?

GROVER. I'm a Satyr! I'm half-goat?

PERCY. *And you couldn't have mentioned that sooner?*

SALLY. Grover... is a Fury after Percy right now?

GROVER. A Fury? Oh, no no no –

SALLY. Oh thank god.

GROVER. It's a Minotaur.

SALLY. Oh no. Grover, you need to get Percy to the border.

PERCY. What about you?

SALLY. You're the one it's after, Percy. *(She kisses him.)* I love you so much.

>*(Lightning flashes. Enter: The **MINOTAUR**. Half-man, half-bull. Sound effects: Minotaur roar!)*

Run!

>*(**SALLY** stands, drawing the **MINOTAUR**'s attention, as **GROVER** tries to pull **PERCY** to safety.)*

GROVER. You heard your mom!

PERCY. I'm not leaving her!

>*(But **PERCY** sees the **MINOTAUR** has trapped **SALLY**. He pulls out the pen he got from **MR. BRUNNER**.)*

If Mrs. Dodds was really a monster, I hope you're really a sword...

>*(The pen expands into a sword.)*

Awesome!

>*(**PERCY** runs to the **MINOTAUR**, wielding the sword. The **MINOTAUR** turns its attention from **SALLY** to **PERCY**...)*

>*(**PERCY** swings the sword. The **MINOTAUR** blocks with his horns. For a tense moment, the two are locked in this position... But the*

MINOTAUR *is stronger. He pushes* **PERCY** *to the ground, injuring him. He advances...)*

SALLY. Over here.

(**SALLY** *steps in the* **MINOTAUR***'s path.*)

You want my son, you have to answer to me.

(*The* **MINOTAUR** *lowers its head and charges* **SALLY**. *It attacks and she falls, lifeless.*)

PERCY. Mom! *Noooo!!!!*

(*He slays the* **MINOTAUR**. *Sound effects:* **MINOTAUR** *scream/roar! As it vanishes, it Hulk-punches him to the ground.* **PERCY** *falls.*)

GROVER. Percy! Don't pass out don't pass out dooon't paaaaass oouuuuutttt –

(**PERCY** *passes out. Silence. Eventually, he rises and moves as if suspended in water.*)

PERCY.	CHORUS.
IS THIS REAL?	OOH
AM I DEAD OR AM I DREAMING?	
AM I UNDERNEATH THE OCEAN,	OOH
OR ARE MY EYES JUST STREAMING?	
THIS IS WEIRD.	OOH

(*A guy in a Hawaiian shirt appears. It's* **POSEIDON**. *But* **PERCY** *doesn't know that yet.*)

PERCY. Oh look, a strange man in a Hawaiian shirt.

(**POSEIDON** *offers* **PERCY** *a seashell.*)

POSEIDON. "What belongs to the sea can always return to the sea." *(Beat.)* It's a seashell.

*(**POSEIDON** disappears.)*

PERCY.

LIKE I SAID, WEIRD.

*(**ANNABETH** appears. She and **PERCY** lock eyes.)*

PERCY.	**CHORUS.**
IS SHE REAL?	OOH
I MUST BE DREAMING.	OOH
SHE'S FLOATING CLOSE	OOH
TO ME	OOH
LIKE AN ANGEL, OR IT'S	
SEEMING.	
THIS IS WEIRD.	
BUT A GOOD WEIRD	
I'VE NEVER SEEN A FACE	AHH
AS BEAUTIFUL AS –	

ANNABETH. You drool when you sleep.

PERCY. Wait, what? Where am I? Where's my mom?

ANNABETH. I should tell Mr. D you're awake. *(As she exits.)* Mr. D!

*(She's gone. **PERCY** takes in his surroundings. He is startled when **MR. D** enters.)*

[MUSIC NO. 04 – ANOTHER TERRIBLE DAY]

MR. D.

OH, YOU'RE ALIVE.

I SUPPOSE THAT'S GOOD NEWS FOR YOU,

BUT IT MEANS A LOT MORE PAPERWORK FOR ME.

SO DON'T EXPECT ME TO BE HAPPY TO SEE YOU.

OF COURSE, BEING ALIVE IS TEMPORARY.

So maybe if I go away and play pinochle for a few hours, things might improve. For me. Not for you. You'd be dead.

PERCY. Where am I?

MR. D.

> GREAT, YOU HAVEN'T BEEN DEBRIEFED.
> THIS IS WAY OUT OF MY PAY GRADE,
> WHICH IS SAYING A LOT,
> 'CAUSE I DON'T GET PAID.

> *(Into his megaphone.)*

> SOMEONE FIND PROFESSOR 'HAY-FOR-BREATH'
> AND TELL HIM PETER JOHNSON IS AWAKE,
> SO HE BETTER CLIP-CLOP OVER HERE!

PERCY. It's Percy Jackson.

MR. D. Whatever!

> JUST ANOTHER TERRIBLE DAY
> AT CAMP HALF-BLOOD,
> WHERE EV'RYTHING'S THE WORST!
> JUST ANOTHER TERRIBLE DAY.
> I'M THE GOD OF WINE AND I'M DYING OF THIRST

PERCY. Wait, did you say you're a *god?*

MR. D. Dionysus, god of wine. Yeah, gods are real. What do you want, a pony?

> *(**MR. BRUNNER** enters.)*

Speaking of ponies.

MR. BRUNNER. Percy!

PERCY. *Mr. Brunner?* What are you doing here? What is going on?!?

MR. BRUNNER. It's complicated –

MR. D.

> OH KID, YOU HAVE NO IDEA
> ABOUT THIS PLACE OR YOUR FORMER MENTOR.
> I DON'T HAVE TIME TO FILL YOU IN ON THE DETAILS,
> BUT LOOK, HE'S ALSO A CENTAUR.

(**MR. D** *whips the blanket off* **MR. BRUNNER**, *revealing he has the lower body of a horse.*)

MR. BRUNNER. *(Sheepish.)* I did mean to tell you...

MR. D.
 ANOTHER TERRIBLE DAY
 STUCK WITH THESE RUNTS IN THE MUCK AND MUD.
 ANOTHER TERRIBLE DAY
 OH GODS!

I need a drink

 ENJOY YOUR STAY AT CAMP HALF-BLOOD.

  (**MR. D** *exits.*)

MR. BRUNNER. You'll get used to Mr. D. He... well. He hates children.

PERCY. Mr. Brunner?

MR. BRUNNER AKA CHIRON. My true name is Chiron. And my real job is training half-bloods. Half-god, half-mortal. Like you.

PERCY. But I'm not... I mean, this has to be a mistake. Let me talk to my mom, she'll clear this up. *(Off* **CHIRON***'s grave look.)* Where is my mom?

CHIRON. Grover said she fought bravely.

[MUSIC NO. 04A – SHE FOUGHT BRAVELY]

But a mortal woman, against a minotaur...

PERCY. It wasn't a dream. She's really gone.

CHIRON. I'm so sorry, Percy.

PERCY. It's my fault. She was trying to protect me.

CHIRON. You mustn't blame yourself.

PERCY. You say the gods are real. So how could they let that happen?

CHIRON. I'm afraid there are some questions only the gods themselves can answer.

[MUSIC NO. 05 – THEIR SIGN]

LOOK FOR THEIR SIGN.
YOU HAVE TO BE PATIENT.
A SIGN THAT THE GODS HAVE A PLAN.
I KNOW THAT THE FUTURE LOOKS BLURRY,
BUT NOT TO WORRY,
JUST DO WHAT YOU CAN.

PERCY. If my dad's a god, I'd like to know which one. He's got a lot to answer for.

HE SHOWED NO SIGN
THAT HE EVER EXISTED.
NO SIGN HE MIGHT ACTU'LLY CARE.
MY MOM RAISED ME ALL ON HER LONESOME,
WHEN I WOULD REACH OUT, NO ONE ELSE WOULD BE
    THERE.

So who is he?

CHIRON. *(Darkly.)* It could be… that is to say… the prophecies suggest… *(A beat as* **PERCY** *waits for an answer. Then, cheerful:)* But that's impossible! I'll see you at dinner, Percy!

> (**CHIRON** *exits.* **LUKE,** *who has been watching from the sidelines, steps forward. He oozes charismatic cool.)*

LUKE. Tough first day?

PERCY. All this time I thought my dad was some deadbeat. Turns out…

LUKE. …he's a dead-beat god. I get how you feel. I was your age when I found out my dad was Hermes, the messenger god. You know, Old Wings-On-His-Shoes?

PERCY. Have you ever met him?

LUKE. *(Beat.)* Look, the gods are busy. They have a lot of kids, and they don't always care. If you're one of the lucky ones…

THEY'LL SEND A SIGN
IF THEY WANT TO CLAIM YOU,
A SIGN TO ADMIT YOU'RE THEIR OWN.

PERCY.

AND IF THEY DON'T?

LUKE.

THEN NO ONE CAN BLAME YOU
FOR HOLDING A GRUDGE,
SO, HEY, *(Laughs.)*
YOU'RE NOT ALONE.

I'm Luke. I'm gonna be your counselor. The Hermes cabin takes anyone who hasn't been claimed. We're literally the reject cabin. Welcome to the dysfunctional family.

PERCY. Thanks, Luke.

LUKE. Come on, you should get some sleep. You've got a big day tomorrow.

PERCY. I just found out everything I ever knew about my life was wrong. What could possibly be bigger than that?

(A whistle blows and **CLARISSE** *runs by, screaming.)*

CLARISSE. Capture the Flag!

*(***PERCY** *and* **LUKE** *enter the grounds to discover* **GROVER.***)*

GROVER. Percy! You're baa-aack!

PERCY. Grover! It's good to see... all of you. Are you ever going to wear pants again?

GROVER. Nope! *(He hands* **PERCY** *a sword and shield.)* This is for you.

PERCY. Why?

ANNABETH. Haven't you played Capture the Flag before?

PERCY. You're my dream girl! I mean... the girl I saw... when I was dreaming...

LUKE. This is Annabeth. Our cabins are on the same team. See, cabins are grouped by parent. And each cabin has certain... gifts. I figure, if we find what you're good at, maybe that'll give us a clue about your dad.

PERCY. I don't have any gifts.

ANNABETH. You have ADHD, right? Dyslexia too?

PERCY. Yeah, but –

ANNABETH. Letters float off the page when you read because your mind is hardwired for ancient Greek. And the ADHD – you're impulsive, you can't sit still in class. Those are your battlefield reflexes.

PERCY. So who's *your* dad?

ANNABETH. He's a history professor.

PERCY. He's human? But I thought...

ANNABETH. My *mom* is Athena. Goddess of wisdom. Sexist much?

PERCY. No! I mean, I love girls! I mean... I think they're really... nice!

GROVER. Then you should meet the captain of the other team.

PERCY. Who's the captain of the other team?

(**CLARISSE** *appears.*)

CLARISSE. *I am.*

[MUSIC NO. 06 – PUT YOU IN YOUR PLACE]

PERCY. Ahh!

LUKE. Meet Clarisse, the daughter of Ares, god of war.

CLARISSE. You got a problem with that? Prepare to be pulverized – *newbie.*

(*To* **PERCY.**) YOU WANNA KNOW WHOSE HOUSE YOU'RE FIGHTING FOR:
THE GOD OF STRATEGY, THE GOD OF WAR,
THE GOD OF WATER, OR THE GOD OF DEATH,
BEFORE YOU TAKE YOUR FINAL BREATH.

(*To* **LUKE.**) GOD OF MESSENGERS, GO TAKE A NOTE:

(*To everyone.*) YOU GONNA DROWN, YOU AIN'T GONNA FLOAT.
YOU GONNA LOSE, YEAH, YOU MISSED THE BOAT.
IT'S GONNA BE BLOODY MURDER SHE WROTE!
I'LL PUT YOU IN,
I'LL PUT YOU IN,
I'LL PUT YOU IN YOUR PLACE.
I'LL PUT YOU IN,
I'LL PUT YOU IN,
I'LL PUT YOU IN YOUR PLACE.

PERCY. We have to beat *her*?

ANNABETH. Don't worry. Athena always has a plan.
EV'RY DEMI HAS A SPECIAL SKILL:

PERCY, GROVER & LUKE.
SPECIAL SKILL...

ANNABETH.
SPEED, OR BRAINS, OR THE STRENGTH OF WILL.

PERCY, GROVER & LUKE.
STRENGTH OF WILL...

ANNABETH.
BUT SHE, SHE'S GONNA TAKE A SPECIAL SPILL-
RIGHT TO THE BOTTOM OF THE BIGGEST HILL.

CLARISSE
I'LL PUT YOU IN,
I'LL PUT YOU IN,

CLARISSE & ANNABETH.
I'LL PUT YOU IN YOUR PLACE!

CLARISSE.
I'LL PUT YOU IN,

ANNABETH.
I'LL PUT YOU IN,

CLARISSE.
I'LL PUT YOU IN,

ANNABETH.
I'LL PUT YOU IN,

CLARISSE & ANNABETH.
I'LL PUT YOU IN YOUR PLACE

GROVER.
OW, OW, OW MY FACE ...

ANNABETH. All right, team. Let's talk strategy. Hermes kids are fast, so Luke?

LUKE. Actually, that's a stereotype – foot brigade, got it.

ANNABETH. Grover? Satyrs are creatures of Pan – god of the wild. You know what to do?

GROVER. Yep. Hide in a tree!

PERCY. What about me? I don't know my talent yet.

ANNABETH. I have a special job for you. Go to the boy's bathroom.

PERCY. And?

ANNABETH. Stay there. It's your first day. We don't want you messing this up.

ALL. Battle!!!

> *(Breakdown! A huge sword fight ensues, all in rhythm, a la Stomp meets "Enter the Dragon". Full cast should be involved, with the Brunner actor now playing a camper on Clarisse's team. In the chaos,* **PERCY** *finds his way to the bathroom.)*

PERCY. Okay. Just stay here. Just stay in the bathroom, and stay out of...

> *(***CLARISSE*** *appears.)*

CLARISSE.
TROUBLE?
HA! HEARD YOU WERE TOUGH,

(Snorts.)

BUT YOU DON'T LOOK IT.

(Smacks her fist.)

YOUR GOOSE IS COOKED.
I'M HERE TO COOK IT.
YOU FACED A MONSTER ON YOUR VERY FIRST DAY.
YOU LUCKY PUNK, NOW NEWBIE, YOU'RE GONNA PAY!
I'LL PUT YOU IN,

CHORUS.
SHE'LL PUT YOU IN,

CLARISSE.
I'LL PUT YOU IN,

CHORUS.
SHE'LL PUT YOU IN,

ALL.

I'LL/SHE'LL PUT YOU IN YOUR PLACE!

> (*They fight.* **CLARISSE** *disarms* **PERCY***, knocking him onto a toilet.*)

CLARISSE.

I'LL PUT YOU IN,

CHORUS.

SHE'LL PUT YOU IN,

CLARISSE.

I'LL PUT YOU IN,

CHORUS.

SHE'LL PUT YOU IN,

ALL.

I'LL/SHE'LL PUT YOU IN YOUR PLACE!

[MUSIC NO. 06A – CLARISSE MAKES A SPLASH]

> (*Sound effects: rumble of water moving through pipes.*)

CLARISSE. What's that noise?

PERCY. It's not me. It's – *THE TOILET!!!*

ALL.

OOH-OOOAAAAAH!!

> (**PERCY** *dives off the toilet, as a stream of water rises from the toilet bowl... and hits* **CLARISSE.** **LUKE** *and* **GROVER** *run in, followed by* **ANNABETH.***)

CLARISSE. *(As she runs out.)* You're worm meat, Jackson! Worm meat!

GROVER. Whoa, what happened here?

PERCY. I ...had... an... accident?

(**LUKE** and **GROVER** crack up laughing.)

LUKE. All hail Percy Jackson, supreme lord of the bathroom!

(Everyone cheers and moves off, leaving **PERCY** and **ANNABETH** alone.)

ANNABETH. Not bad for your first day.

PERCY. You set me up. You told me to hide in the bathroom. You knew Clarisse would go after me. I was part of your plan!

ANNABETH. You mean distracting Ares' best warrior so I could capture their flag? Smart plan.

PERCY. She could've killed me!

ANNABETH. The plan would've worked either way. So how'd you drench Clarisse the beast anyway?

PERCY. I don't know, it was like the water in the toilet just responded to me...

(**ANNABETH** is staring at him, suddenly scared.)

What?

ANNABETH. I really hope that doesn't mean what I think it means...

[MUSIC NO. 06B – THE TRIDENT APPEARS/THUNDER]

(The others run in, looking at the sky.)

LUKE. Check it out! The stars!

PERCY. What's going on?

LUKE. I told you, sometimes the gods send a sign.

PERCY. Is that a... fork?

CHIRON. It's a trident. I galloped here as soon as I could. It seems your godly parent has claimed you after all. All hail Perseus Jackson, Son of the Sea God – Poseidon.

PERCY. My dad's *Poseidon?* Oh *sweet!*

> *(But everyone is staring at him in horror.)*

... What?

> *(Sound effects: thunder, rain. Campers scatter to get out of the storm.* **LUKE** *goes to* **PERCY**.*)*

Luke. What's going on?

LUKE. Mr. D. wants to kill you. I mean talk to you.

> *(***LUKE** *leads* **PERCY** *to* **CHIRON** *and* **MR. D** *in the Big House.)*

PERCY. I don't get it, what did I do wrong?

MR. D. You were born.

CHIRON. Mr. D ...

MR. D. No! He deserves to know! The Big Three gods aren't supposed to have kids!

PERCY. The Big Three?

CHIRON. Kronos' most powerful sons. Zeus, Hades... *(Pointed.)* and Poseidon.

MR. D. And you know why? *Because they're always trouble.* Now Zeus's favorite toy is stolen right before you turn up... and the big guy thinks YOU did it!

PERCY. Wait, what does Zeus think I stole?

CHIRON. His lightning.

PERCY. His *lightning?*

MR. D. And not some crummy tin-foil zig-zag from a Broadway musical. We're talking two feet of celestial bronze, capped with god-level explosives. And the only one who could take it… *is a half-blood!*

PERCY. I didn't take anything!

CHIRON. We know that.

PERCY. So what happens to me now?

CHIRON. You must go to the attic.

[MUSIC NO. 07 – THE ORACLE]

Speak to our mummy.

PERCY. When you say "mummy" … that's like old person for "mom," right?

CHIRON. Be brave, Percy. Because if you fail… all the gods will be at war.

> (*Sound effects: Creepy transition.* **CHIRON** *and* **MR. D** *exit.*)

> (*Transition to: the attic. It's spooky.*)

PERCY. Is anyone up here – AAAH!!!

> (*A mummified woman appears:* **THE ORACLE**.)

ORACLE. *Approach, child, and face your destiny.*
YOU SHALL GO WEST AND FACE THE TREACH'ROUS LORD.

ECHOES.
WEST AND FACE THE TREACH'ROUS LORD.

ORACLE.
YOU SHALL FIND WHAT WAS STOLEN AND SEE IT RESTORED.

ECHOES.
SAFELY RESTORED.

PERCY. Really? Okay, that's great! That's –

ORACLE.
> YOU SHALL BE BETRAYED BY ONE WHO CALLS YOU
> FRIEND.

PERCY.
> WAIT, WHAT!?!

ORACLE.
> AND YOU SHALL FAIL

ECHOES.
> FAIL!

ORACLE.
> TO SAVE WHAT MATTERS MOST

ORACLE & ECHOES.
> IN THE END.

> *(Later.* **PERCY** *is in the Big House with* **CHIRON**, **LUKE**, **ANNABETH**, *and* **GROVER**.*)*

CHIRON. "Go west to face the treacherous lord."

LUKE. It's got to mean Hades, right?

PERCY. Why Hades?

GROVER. The Underworld is in Los Angeles.

PERCY. Actually, I'm not surprised.

CHIRON. Hades has always been jealous of his brothers. If he stole the lightning bolt to start a war between Zeus and Poseidon, then you have to stop him.

PERCY. Me?

ANNABETH. A hero's quest. It's only the biggest honor a half-blood can get.

> *(***ANNABETH** *storms off.)*

LUKE. Annabeth's right. Your dad needs a hero to clear his name. This quest could be the whole reason he claimed you.

PERCY. Where was he when I got kicked out of school? Or when we couldn't pay the rent? Or when my mom... Forget it. I'm staying here.

(**CHIRON** *and the others exchange a look.*)

CHIRON. I'm afraid that's not an option. I'm sorry, Percy. As long as you're here, Zeus will punish the entire camp. Which means...

PERCY. You're going to expel me. Again.

CHIRON. I wish there was another way.

[MUSIC NO. 08 – GOOD KID]

(**CHIRON** *exits. After a concerned look back at* **PERCY**, **LUKE** *follows him out.* **GROVER** *is the last to go.*)

PERCY.
SIX SCHOOLS IN SIX YEARS.
BEEN KICKED OUT OF EV'RY PLACE.
EV'RYTHING I EVER DO IS WRONG.
NEVER FIND WHERE I BELONG,
EV'RYBODY ON MY CASE.

THE SAME OLD STORY.
THE SAME OLD SONG:
DON'T ACT UP,
DON'T ACT OUT.
BE STRONG.

I KEEP MY HEAD DOWN.
I KEEP MY CHIN UP.
BUT IT ENDS UP ALL THE SAME, WITH:

PERCY & CHORUS.
"PACK YOUR BAGS, PERCY,
YOU'RE ALWAYS TO BLAME!"

PERCY.	**CHORUS.**
I NEVER TRY TO DO ANYTHING.	AH
I NEVER MEANT TO HURT ANYONE.	AH AH
I TRY, I TRY TO BE A GOOD KID	AH
A GOOD KID	
A GOOD SON.	OOH
BUT NO ONE EVER WILL TAKE MY SIDE,	OOH AH
ALL I EVER DO IS	AH

PERCY & CHORUS.

TAKE THE FALL

PERCY.

I SWEAR, I SWEAR THAT I'M A GOOD KID.
GUESS I'M GOOD FOR NOTHING AT –
ALL THE SCHOOLS IN SIX YEARS.
EV'RY BATTLE, EV'RY DAY,
NO ONE EVER TELLS ME THAT THEY'RE PROUD.
NO ONE ASKS ME, "PERCY, HOW'D YOU LIKE TO COME
    AROUND AND STAY?"
ALL YOU GET ARE
BAD GRADES,
AND A BUM RAP,
AND A BAD REP,
AND A GOOD SMACK,
AND NO FRIENDS,
AND NO HOPE,
AND NO MOM...
SHE'S TAKEN AWAY.

(**PERCY** *feels truly abandoned. He sinks.*)

I SWEAR I NEVER STOLE ANYTHING.
I NEVER MEANT TO HURT ANYONE.

I SWEAR, I SWEAR THAT I'M A GOOD KID,
A GOOD KID WHO'S HAD A BAD RUN.
AND ALL I NEED IS ONE LAST CHANCE
TO PROVE I'M GOOD ENOUGH FOR SOMEONE.

(He rises.)

I'M GOOD ENOUGH FOR SOMEONE

CHORUS.
SIX SCHOOLS IN SIX YEARS.
SIX SCHOOLS IN SIX YEARS.

PERCY.
I'M GOOD ENOUGH FOR SOMEONE.

CHORUS.
SIX SCHOOLS IN SIX YEARS.

*(**LUKE** appears.)*

LUKE. Pro tip. When you're the son of Poseidon and you want to be alone… don't go to the lake. *(He sits with* **PERCY.***)* I get it. The gods don't care about us, or if we get hurt. If it were my dad, I wouldn't go either.

PERCY. It's not just that. The Oracle said I'd be betrayed by a friend. That even if I find the bolt, I'll fail.

LUKE. Hey, prophecies don't always mean what you think they mean. And I'm not gonna say you owe your dad anything because you don't. But your mom…

PERCY. My mom's gone.

LUKE. From this world. But if she's anywhere… she'd be in…

[MUSIC NO. 09 – KILLER QUEST!]

PERCY. …the Underworld. *(Beat.)*

YEAH, I'LL DO IT!
NOT 'CAUSE MY DAD NEEDS ME.

HE'S BEEN LESS A DAD AND MORE ABSENTEE.
BUT IF MY MOM'S ALIVE, THAT'S WHERE SHE'S BOUND TO BE.
I'M LEAVING NOW, I'D BETTER PACK.
HADES TOOK MY MOM, I'M TAKING HER BACK.

(**GROVER** *appears.*)

GROVER. And I'm coming with you.
YOU'RE MY BEST FRIEND, DUDE. SO DON'T GET MAD,
BUT I SUSPECT YOU'LL NEED PROTECTING WHEN THINGS
GET *(Goat bleat.)* BAAAD!
AND THIS KICKIN' QUEST MAY BE THE BEST CHANCE I'VE
    HAD
TO PUT MY PAST BEHIND ME. SO IF YOU HAVEN'T
    GUESSED
I'M GOING ON YOUR KILLER QUEST!

PERCY. *(With resolve.)*
SO BON VOYAGE AND FARE ME WELL,

GROVER.
WE'RE GONNA FIGHT EACH FOE, EACH CURSE AND SPELL.

PERCY.
WE'RE GONNA MARCH STRAIGHT DOWN TO THE GATES
    OF HELL!

LUKE. Underworld.

PERCY. Close enough.

(**ANNABETH** *enters.*)

ANNABETH. I'm coming too, Seaweed Brain. (**PERCY**
mouths to **GROVER***: "Seaweed brain?".)* If you're going
to save the world, I'm the best person to keep you from
messing up.

FIVE LONG YEARS STUCK AT CAMP,
UNDERNEATH ATHENA'S LOCKED DOWN CLAMP.
BEEN WAITIN' FOR MY CHANCE TO PROVE I'M CHAMP.

> I'VE GOT MAD BATTLE STRATEGY, MY MOM WILL BE
> IMPRESSED.
> I'M COMING ON YOUR KILLER QUEST!

PERCY, GROVER & ANNABETH.
> SO BLAST THE HORNS, GET THE FLAGS UNFURLED,
> PAST DANGERS, SLINGS AND ARROWS HURLED!
> WE'RE GONNA MARCH STRAIGHT DOWN TO THE
> UNDERWORLD!

LUKE. How about something for the road?

> *(***LUKE*** *hands* **PERCY** *a pair of winged shoes.)*

PERCY. Shoes with wings! Awesome!

> *(***CHIRON*** *and* **CLARISSE** *arrive to see them off.)*

CLARISSE. Don't get eaten by monsters.

PERCY. Wait, who said anything about monsters –

GROVER. Los Angeles, here we come!

> *(The camp waves them goodbye.)*

ALL. *(Campers.)*
> WE'RE /YOU'RE GOING ON AN AWESOME –

PERCY.
> DANGEROUS AND SCARY!

ALL.
> THRILLING –

ANNABETH.
> MONSTEROUS!

GROVER.
> AND HAIRY!

ALL.
> KILLER HERO'S QUEST!

(They land at a pine tree. Sound effects: thunder, rain.)

ANNABETH. This is it. Once we go past this tree, we're officially outside the camp border. Every monster on the east coast will be hunting for us.

PERCY. Great. *(Beat.)* You go first.

ANNABETH. What, me? It's your quest.

PERCY. Grover?

GROVER. Maybe we should do this together. *(They approach the border, and take a breath.)* One...

ANNABETH. Two...

PERCY. Three!

> *(They step across the border and look around.)*

It's not so scary. *(Off a creepy noise, he immediately panics.)* What was that?

ANNABETH. Relax, Seaweed Brain. I'll take care of it. Whatever you do...don't do anything.

> *(She exits.)*

PERCY. She's kind of intense.

GROVER. She's right. The world is full of monsters, and monsters hunt people like us. The only place we're safe is at camp.

PERCY. Like, the gods protect us there?

GROVER. The gods don't protect us. The tree does.

> *(**PERCY** laughs – then stops when he sees **GROVER**'s face.)*

PERCY. You're...not joking.

GROVER. I wish I were.

[MUSIC NO. 10 – THE TREE ON THE HILL]

THERE'S A TREE ON THE HILL, UP ON HALF-BLOOD HILL,
THAT WATCHES OVER US, SILENT AND STILL.
AND NO ONE AT CAMP IS SAFE UNTIL
WE CAN SEE THE TREE ON THE HILL.

(**ANNABETH** *and* **LUKE** *appear, as kids.*)

The first time I saw it… I was taking three half-bloods
to camp. Annabeth, Luke…

PERCY.

And the other one?

GROVER.

Her name was Thalia. Tough
    girl. (**THALIA** *appears.*)
    Like her father… Zeus.

PERCY.

I thought I was the only kid
    of the Big Three Gods.

GROVER.

You are now.

CHORUS.

OOO

OOO

(*Suddenly, we're in a flashback:* **GROVER,**
LUKE, ANNABETH, *and* **THALIA** *in the woods.*)

THALIA. Grover! Which way?

GROVER. That way! Wait. Is that north?

(*A* **CYCLOPS** *appears.*)

CYCLOPS. *I … smell… half-bloods…*

ANNABETH. Cyclops!!

LUKE. Run!

GROVER.
> AND THERE ON THE HILL, UP ON HALF-BLOOD HILL
> WE RAN AND FOUGHT WITH SPEED AND SKILL;
> FOR NOTHING WOULD SLAKE ITS WRATHFUL WILL.
> WE HAD TO MAKE A STAND –

THALIA. *(To* **GROVER.***)* Get the others to safety.

GROVER. I'm not leaving you.

> (**THALIA** *turns back to confront the* **CYCLOPS** *alone.)*

> AND MAYBE IF I'D BEEN A LITTLE BIT BRAVER.
> MAYBE IF I'D STAYED BEHIND TO FIGHT.
> BUT "MAYBE" DOESN'T LET ME GO BACK AND SAVE HER.
> "MAYBE" DOESN'T MAKE IT ALRIGHT.

PERCY. So what happened?!?

GROVER. That's when Zeus showed up.

PERCY. And saved her... right?

GROVER.
> It was too late for that.
>   As she died,
> he turned her into a
>   tree. <u>That</u> tree.
> So she could stand
> protecting us, forever.
> The way I couldn't do
>   for her...

LUKE & ANNABETH.
> OOH
> AAH

> (**LUKE** *and* **ANNABETH** *watch as* **THALIA** *transforms into a tree.)*

ANNABETH. Thalia...

LUKE. We won't forget you. We promise.

GROVER.
> THERE'S A TREE ON THE HILL, UP ON HALF-BLOOD HILL,
> THAT PROTECTS US ALL, AND ALWAYS WILL.

(**LUKE** *and* **ANNABETH** *disappear.*)

AND IT'S THERE REMINDING ME
OF ALL I FAILED TO BE
THE TREE ON THE HILL.

PERCY. Hey... I'm glad you're here. *(The* **CHORUS** *makes a hissing sound.)* Do you hear something?

[MUSIC NO. 10A – A VISIT WITH AUNTY EM]

(**AUNTY EM** *appears. She wears sunglasses and a Grey Gardens-style turban hiding her hair.*)

AUNTY EM. Children! It's too late to be out all alone.

PERCY. We're fine, ma'am, we're just... Camping.

AUNTY EM. In a storm like this? Poor dears! Come inside, Aunty Em will find you a place to stay.

PERCY. She seems nice.

(*They follow her in. The* **CHORUS** *acts as statues.*)

Wow. Did you make all these statues yourself?

AUNTY EM. Everyone needs a hobby.

GROVER. That one looks like my Uncle Ferdinand.

PERCY. That one looks like Annabeth. *(Because it is* **ANNABETH**. *She coughs.)* Oh! Annabeth!

ANNABETH. We're leaving. Now.

AUNTY EM. Wait. *(A snake-like hissing from the* **CHORUS**.*)* Your eyes are quite unique, my dear.

ANNABETH. ...Really?

GROVER. *(Re: Uncle Ferdinand.)* Seriously. The detail work is amazing!

AUNTY EM. Would you mind if I took your picture? I'd like to create a new statue.

ANNABETH. *(Flattered.)* Of me?

AUNTY EM. You deserve to be immortalized in stone forever.

> *(The hissing grows louder.)*

PERCY. Does anyone else hear a hissing sound?

GROVER. Yep, she really captured Uncle Ferdinand!

AUNTY EM. Who's ready for their close-up?

GROVER. Really... captured...

ANNABETH. Don't you need a camera?

AUNTY EM. Why use a camera...

GROVER. Percy! That IS Uncle Ferdinand!

AUNTY EM. *...when you have a face like mine?*

ANNABETH. Close your eyes! Aunty <u>M</u>! For –

> **(ANNABETH** *and* **PERCY** *close their eyes, just as* **AUNTY EM** *throws off her turban and sunglasses, revealing her hair is made of writhing snakes.)*

AUNTY EM AKA MEDUSA. *Medussssa! And your mother and I are old nemesissss... Nemesessss... Nemissississss... We don't like each other.*

PERCY. Annabeth, run!

> *(Eyes closed,* **PERCY** *swings his sword wildly. Of course, he misses.* **MEDUSA** *laughs.)*

AUNTY EM AKA MEDUSA. *Sssssuch a brave hero. Jussst like your father. But trussst me, your quesssst ends here –*

CHORUS.
    AHHH

(Sound effects: **PERCY***'s sword connects and* **MEDUSA***'s head falls off.)*

PERCY. What just happened?

*(***ANNABETH*** cautiously opens her eyes.)*

ANNABETH. You can open your eyes. But don't look directly at her. She can still turn you to stone, even *after* you've chopped off her head.

PERCY. *(As he opens his eyes in horror.)* I chopped off her *head??*

ANNABETH. None of this would've happened if you'd stayed where I told you!

PERCY. Me? You're the one she was after! What does she have against your mom anyway?

ANNABETH. *(Reluctant.)* Medusa used to be beautiful, until Athena... turned her into a monster.

PERCY. She did WHAT?

GROVER. I'll be over here.

*(***GROVER*** exits.)*

ANNABETH. Medusa disrespected her! She was sneaking into Athena's temple to meet up with her boyfriend... *(Pointed.)* Poseidon. Yeah, Medusa dated your dad.

PERCY. Is that why you don't like me? Because our parents don't like each other?

ANNABETH. I never said I don't like you.

PERCY. You criticize me. All the time.

ANNABETH. Look. I've studied, I've trained, I've done everything to prove to the gods that I'm the best. And you show up and – you don't even know how to hold a sword.

(**PERCY** *grabs his sword.*)

PERCY. Yes I do. *(He hits himself with sword.)* Ow.

ANNABETH. *(She corrects his grip.)* Hands here.

PERCY. You're smart, you're brave... how could your mom not be proud of you?

ANNABETH. That's what I want to know.

[MUSIC NO. 11 – MY GRAND PLAN]

I'VE ALWAYS BEEN A SMART GIRL.
ALWAYS MADE THE GRADE,
ALWAYS GOT THE GOLD STAR.
I'VE ALWAYS BEEN A SMART GIRL.
BUT "SMART GIRL" ONLY GETS A GIRL SO FAR.
YOU WIN AT EV'RY SINGLE GAME.
YOU WANT A QUEST, THEY TELL YOU, "TOUGH."
IF YOU DON'T GO
YOU'LL NEVER KNOW
IF YOU'LL EVER BE GOOD ENOUGH!
MY GRAND PLAN
IS THAT I WILL BE REMEMBERED.
MY GRAND PLAN,
JUST YOU WAIT AND SEE!
THEY BETTER WISE UP, 'CAUSE I'LL RISE UP.
BRING ON ANY CHALLENGE,
AND SOMEDAY SOON SOMEONE
WILL NOTICE ME.

PERCY. I know what it's like to not feel good enough. You know how many times I've been kicked out of school?

ANNABETH. Yeah, but when boys screw up, they always get another chance.

I'VE ALWAYS BEEN A TOUGH GIRL.
ALWAYS BEEN THE ONE NOT TO RUN FROM A FIGHT.
ALWAYS BEEN A TOUGH GIRL,
'CAUSE MOST GIRLS NEVER WIN IF THEY'RE POLITE.

SO ME, I TEND TO STAND MY GROUND.
I FOUND I NEVER CAN GIVE IN.
IT MAY NOT BE MY QUEST,
BUT MAYBE IT'S MINE TO WIN!

BUT YOUR STEPMOM TREATS YOU LIKE SOME FREAK.
AND YOUR DAD WON'T GIVE YOU THE TIME OF DAY.
AND YOUR MOM WON'T TRUST YOU WITH A QUEST,
SO THE BEST THING YOU CAN DO IS RUN AWAY!
RUN AWAY...

BUT I HAVE A PLAN,
AND I WILL BE REMEMBERED.
I WILL BE GREAT.
JUST WAIT AND SEE.
THEY BETTER WISE UP, 'CAUSE I'LL RISE UP.
BRING ON ANY CHALLENGE,
AND SOMEDAY SOON I SWEAR,
I DON'T KNOW HOW OR WHEN,
BUT I PROMISE YOU,
I'LL NEVER BE INVISIBLE AGAIN.
SOMEONE WILL NOTICE ME.

>   (**PERCY** and **ANNABETH** *share a moment.*)

I'VE ALWAYS BEEN A SMART GIRL.

>   (*The song ends.* **PERCY** *takes a box and shoves* **MEDUSA***'s head inside.*)

PERCY. No more fighting?

ANNABETH. At least not with each other.

PERCY. Come on. I know how to get our parents to notice us. Help me box up this head. *(Writes on box.)* Hermes Express Shipping. To: Mount Olympus. Care of: Perseus Jackson and Annabeth Chase.

ANNABETH. The gods will think we're impertinent.

PERCY. We *are* impertinent.

(**GROVER** *enters, beaming.*)

GROVER. Guys! I solved all our problems! While you two were here not solving all our problems, look what I found!

PERCY. Three Greyhound tickets!

GROVER. We are totally killing this quest.

[MUSIC NO. 12 – DRIVE]

(*They board a Greyhound bus.*)

BUS DRIVER. Now leaving scenic New Jersey!

GROVER.
GUYS, WE GOT THIS,
YOU AIN'T SHOT THIS.
YO, I KNOW YOUR TRAIN OF THOUGHT IS
THAT THERE AIN'T NO WAY IN HADES THAT WE'LL WIN.

> (**MRS. DODDS** *attacks the bus with her two sister Furies.*)

ANNABETH. Furies!

MRS. DODDS. *Die, Percy Jackson!*

> (*Our Trio fights the Furies off as* **GROVER** *sings.*)

GROVER.
ALL YOUR WORRIES
COME IN FLURRIES
BUT WE'RE BEATING FREAKING FURIES!
LOOK HOW FAR WE'VE COME,
WE CAN'T GIVE IN.

BUS DRIVER. St. Louis!

> (*They get off the bus.*)

GROVER.
IT'S ONE FOOT FORWARD AT A TIME.
DUST OFF ALL THAT GRIT AND GRIME,
WE STILL GOT A LOT LEFT TO DO,
'CAUSE PEOPLE ARE COUNTING ON US
AND I'M COUNTING ON YOU.

UBER DRIVER. Hop in my Uber!

GROVER, PERCY & ANNABETH.
DRIVE, JUST DRIVE!
STAY AHEAD, STAY AHEAD, AND STAY ALIVE.

(The Uber is attacked by a **CHIMERA**.*)*

GROVER.
DUDE, DON'T MEAN TO SCARE YA,
BUT I THINK THAT'S A CHIMERA!

ALL THREE.
AH! PEDAL TO THE METAL
AND DRIVE.

UBER DRIVER. That thing ate my car!

PERCY. We'll give you five stars.

ANNABETH. *Now* how are we going to get to Los Angeles?

*(***ARES** *appears, a war god in biker gear.)*

ARES. How about a ride... from a god? Ares, god of war. Maybe you've met my daughter. Clarisse?

(They all draw their weapons.)

Relax, I come in peace. I hear you runts are headed to Hades. But you'll never make it on public transportation. I can take you as far as Vegas. Y'all cool with motorcycles, right?

(The trio convenes.)

PERCY. What do you think? Can we trust this guy?

GROVER.
IT'S ONE FOOT FORWARD AT A TIME.

PERCY.
DUST OFF ALL THAT GRIT AND GRIME?

ANNABETH.
WE STILL

ALL THREE.
GOT A LOT LEFT TO DO,
'CAUSE PEOPLE ARE COUNTING ON US
AND I'M COUNTING ON YOU.

(A motorcycle revs up. They ride it.)

GROVER, PERCY, & ANNABETH.
DRIVE,

ARES.
DRIVE, DRIVE,

ALL FOUR.
JUST DRIVE!
STAY AHEAD, STAY AHEAD, AND STAY ALIVE.

ARES.
THE ROAD, IT OFFERS FREEDOM,
AS FOR RULES, WELL, WE DON'T NEED 'EM!

ALL THREE & ARES.
SO PEDAL TO THE METAL
AND DRIVE.

ARES. Vegas, baby!

GROVER. Thanks for the ride.

ARES. *(They climb off.)* Don't forget your backpack.

> (**ARES** *tosses* **PERCY** *his backpack and screeches away.)*

GROVER. That guy is so cool.

ANNABETH. OK, gang, we'll be in L.A. tomorrow. But tonight we need a place to sleep.

PERCY. How about here? The Lotus Hotel.

ANNABETH. You're joking, right? In The Odyssey, if you went to sleep in a lotus bed, one night could last one hundred years!

PERCY. I'm sure that's irrelevant. *(He stops* **BIANCA**, *dressed in 1930's fashion.)* Excuse me, miss, how long have <u>you</u> been at this hotel?

BIANCA. Why, my brother and I arrived just yesterday: May 1st... *(***PERCY** *looks at* **ANNABETH***: See?)* 1939.

PERCY. We can sleep on the road!

(They can't get away fast enough.)

ANNABETH, PERCY & GROVER.
DRIVE, JUST DRIVE!
STAY AHEAD, DON'T GET DEAD, AND STAY ALIVE.

GROVER.
WITH THE WIND UPON OUR FACES,
WE'RE GETTING ALL THE PLACES!

ANNABETH.
NO MAJOR FENDER BENDERS,
NOW WE'RE LOOKING LIKE CONTENDERS!

PERCY.
THE ORACLE CAN CAN IT,
I'LL SAVE MY MOM THEN SAVE THE PLANET!

ALL.
SO PEDAL TO THE METAL AND –

PERCY. Look, a convenient bus to Los Angeles!

ALL.
AND DRIVE!

(*They collapse on the bus, exhausted.*)

ANNABETH. Just think, this time tomorrow, we'll be at the Underworld.

GROVER. Yeah, then all we have to do is find Hades, get the bolt back, and stop a bunch of gods from starting a war. We have a plan for that, right?

PERCY. We'll figure it out in the morning. I'm ready to pass out

[MUSIC NO 13 – THE WEIRDEST DREAM (REPRISE)]

paaassss ouutttt paaaaaaaassssss ouuuuuuutttttt...

(**PERCY** *wakes up in the Underworld. Sound effects: drips and cavern sounds.*)

THIS IS STRANGE.
I THINK I MUST BE DREAMING?

(*A creepy musical sting.*)

Scary.

(*A large pit appears. There's something down there, speaking in a deep rumbling voice.*)

VOICE OF KRONOS.
WHERE IS THE BOLT?

(*A shadowy figure approaches the pit. It's* **LUKE**, *but his identity shouldn't be obvious.*)

LUKE. The bolt is on its way, my lord. Everything is unfolding as I – as *we* planned.

VOICE OF KRONOS. *YOU FALTER.*

LUKE. It's nothing. *(Beat.)* The delivery requires certain... sacrifices.

VOICE OF KRONOS.
SACRIFICE IS NECESSARY TO REMAKE THE WORLD. REMEMBER WHAT THESE GODS HAVE DONE. REMEMBER THALIA. AND WHEN I AM FREE – WAIT. SOMEONE IS HERE, LISTENING EVEN AS HE DREAMS. HELLO, PERSEUS JACKSON.

> *(It laughs, horribly, as we hear the sound of something rising from the pit.)*

PERCY.
AAH!!

> **(PERCY** *bolts awake, still on the bus.)*

GROVER. You really do drool in your sleep.

PERCY. Wha? Where are we?

ANNABETH. We're almost at the Underworld.

PERCY. Guys, I had this dream, I was on the edge of this pit, and the thief was there. We've been so sure Hades is behind this. What if we're wrong?

> *(Sound effects: The bus comes to a halt.)*

GROVER. We're about to find out. Are we ready to do this?

PERCY. Not at all. Let's go.

[MUSIC NO. 13A – HELLEVATOR]

> *(They get off the bus and arrive at DOA Records.)*

This must be it.

GROVER. Kinda figured there'd be monsters.

PERCY. Yeah, who knew the lobby of the Underworld would be so...

> (*Sound effects: ding! An elevator opens to reveal* **CHARON**.)

CHARON. Dead? (*He smiles.*) Going down?

ANNABETH. (*To* **PERCY** *and* **GROVER**.) That's Charon, the ferryman to the Underworld. (*To* **CHARON**.) We need to get to Hades.

CHARON. Step inside. No sobs, no screaming, no throwing up.

PERCY. Why would you throw up in an elevator –

> (*Sound effects: The elevator plummets at super speed.*)

ALL THREE.
AHH!!!!

> (*The elevator reaches the bottom. Sound effects: ding!* **CHARON** *shoves them out.*)

CHARON. Enjoy eternity.

[MUSIC NO. 13B – IT'S THE PITS]

> (**CHARON** *vanishes. The trio looks around in the dark, as we hear ghostly whispers from the* **CHORUS**.)

ANNABETH. C'mon, we have to find Hades. Stay close. (**PERCY** *jerks away from her.*) What did I just say?

PERCY. Sorry, I don't know what came over me.

ANNABETH. We have to be careful. If we get separated, we may never find each other again, so – (**PERCY** *jerks away again.*) Seriously?!?

PERCY. I can't help it! It's like my feet won't listen to my brain!

ANNABETH. Well, tell your brain to do something!

PERCY. I swear, it's not me! It's – my – shoes! They're trying to pull me into that piiiiiit!

> *(Sure enough, **PERCY**'s winged shoes have taken on a life of their own. They carry him to the edge of a pit.)*

GROVER. Percy!

> *(**GROVER** and **ANNABETH** try to grab **PERCY**.)*

ANNABETH. Whoa! Gotcha! *(But now all three are pulled towards the pit.)* Take off your shoes!

PERCY. I'm a little – AH! – preoccupied!

GROVER. I'm on it.

> *(**GROVER** busies himself at **PERCY**'s feet. Finally, he rises proudly, holding the shoes.)*

Chewed 'em off. *(They squirm in his hands.)* Whoa! In you go...

> *(He tosses the shoes into the pit. They echo as they flutter down. Silence. Then: a horrible roar. The sound of something big and angry.)*

VOICE OF KRONOS. *PEEEERRRRCCCCYYYY.*

> *(But then it's gone.)*

PERCY. What *was* that?

ANNABETH. Guys... I think this pit is Tartarus.

PERCY. Like... the fish sauce?

ANNABETH. Tatar*us*. After our parents overthrew their father, Kronos, this is where they trapped him.

PERCY. But that doesn't make sense! What would Kronos want with my shoes?

(**ANNABETH** *pulls off* **PERCY***'s backpack.*)

ANNABETH. Unless it wasn't the shoes he was after...

(**ANNABETH** *opens the backpack to reveal a glowing lightning bolt. Sound effects: electric hum.*)

GROVER. That's Zeus's lightning bolt...

PERCY. But why would it be in my... <u>No.</u> You can't think – I didn't steal it, I swear!

ANNABETH. Then someone set us up. But it's not Hades. We need to get out of here before he finds us.

(**HADES** *enters, with flair.*)

HADES. It's too late for that.

[MUSIC NO. 13C – HELLO HADES]

You're as rash as your father, Son of Poseidon. And from the looks of it, as stupid.

PERCY. You know who we are?

HADES. And I know why you're here. You thought I was the bad guy. Everyone always thinks Hades is the bad guy! Maybe it's the décor.

PERCY. Look, you were framed. So was I. If you just let us go –

HADES. One does not simply walk out of the Underworld! That's the whole point of the Underworld! *(Beat.)* Unless...

PERCY. Unless what?

HADES. You give me that bolt. *(He lets this land.)* I may not have stolen it. But since it's here...

PERCY. My father needs this. We're not giving it to you.

HADES. Not even in exchange... for her?

[MUSIC NO. 13D – SALLY APPEARS]

(He waves a hand and **SALLY** *appears.)*

SALLY. Percy?

PERCY. Mom? Mom!

HADES. What has your father ever done for you? He doesn't care about his family, or his brother, who he never visits. He's too busy playing with dolphins, and thinking he's so cool in his Hawaiian shirt.

PERCY. Did you say Hawaiian shirt?

HADES. I can give you your mother back. All it will cost is that bolt. The choice is yours, Son of Poseidon. I'll give you a moment to consider.

[MUSIC NO. 14 – SON OF POSEIDON]

PERCY.
SEEMS MY GOOD INTENTIONS ALWAYS CRASH AND BURN.
EV'RYTHING I TRY TO DO WILL FAIL.
NEVER ONCE WILL I PREVAIL,
GOING WRONG AT EV'RY TURN.

SALLY.
WHAT BELONGS TO THE SEA CAN ALWAYS RETURN.

PERCY & SALLY.
WHAT BELONGS TO THE SEA CAN ALWAYS RETURN.

PERCY. *(Remembering.)* It's a seashell. No… It's a gift from a god.
MAYBE MY DAD WAS A SCREW UP TOO,
HIS BEST LAID PLANS ALWAYS FALLING THROUGH.
MAYBE HE DID THE BEST THAT HE COULD DO.
AND I KNOW RIGHT NOW THINGS ARE LESS THAN FINE.
BUT I THINK MY DAD MAY HAVE THROWN ME A LINE.
AND BETTER LATE THEN NEVER
TO FINALLY GET A SIGN!

(He pulls out the seashell.)

I'M THE SON OF POSEIDON,
AND I AM GONNA WIN!
THE SON OF POSEIDON,
AND I'M DONE RUNNIN'.

Guys, I know how to get us out of here! I'll come back for you, mom. I promise.

(Sound effects: **PERCY** *blows the seashell and a portal appears.)*

GROVER. It's a portal!

HADES. Oh, come on!

(They go through the portal and end up on a beach. Sound effects: ocean waves.)

PERCY. I know who set us up. Who wins if the gods go to war?

ANNABETH. *(Realizing.)* Ares, the God of War.

GROVER. He must have planted the bolt in your backpack!

PERCY. I bet he's watching us right now. *(Calling out to the sky.)* Show yourself!

*(***ARES** *suddenly appears with a baseball bat.)*

ARES.
HA!
YOUR MOUTH'S TALKIN' TRASH,
YOU BETTER RINSE IT.
YOUR MEAT IS MINCED
I'M HERE TO MINCE IT.
I'M GONNA HAVE MY WAR, NOW GIMME SOME SPACE.
I'M GONNA WIPE THAT STUPID HEAD OFF OF YOUR
　　STUPID FACE!

*(They battle **ARES** on the beach.)*

PERCY.	ARES.	GROVER & ANNABETH.
I'M THE SON OF POSEIDON,	I'LL PUT YOU IN!	
	I'LL PUT YOU IN.	WE'LL PUT YOU IN,
		WE'LL PUT YOU IN.
AND I AM GONNA WIN!	I'LL PUT YOU IN YOUR PLACE!	WE'LL PUT YOU IN YOUR PLACE!
THE SON OF POSEIDON,	I'LL PUT YOU IN!	
	I'LL PUT YOU IN.	WE'LL PUT YOU IN,
		WE'LL PUT YOU IN,
AND I'M DONE RUNNIN'	I'LL PUT YOU IN YOUR PLACE!	WE'LL PUT YOU IN YOUR PLACE!

ANNABETH. Percy, get to the ocean!

ARES. You think the god of war is afraid of a little water?

PERCY. How do you feel about a lot of it?

PERCY.	CHORUS.
I'M THE SON OF POSEIDON. I NEVER ASKED TO BE. BUT I'M	AH!

PERCY & CHORUS.
THE SON OF POSEIDON.

PERCY.
NOW FACE THE TIDE
INSIDE ME!

CHORUS.
AH!

[MUSIC NO. 14A – POSEIDON FINALLY SHOWS UP]

(Sound effects: A giant tidal wave washes **ARES** *away.)*

ARES.

NOOOOO!!!

GROVER. That was awesome!

ANNABETH. How did you do that?

(Music plays as **POSEIDON** *enters.)*

POSEIDON. He's a true son of the sea. And the sea does not like to be restrained.

PERCY. Dad. I mean, Lord Poseidon.

POSEIDON. You can call me Dad, Perseus.

PERCY. You can call me Percy. *(Beat.)* I got your gift.

POSEIDON. I got yours. *(He holds up a box.)* Medusa's head?

PERCY. Yeahh, about that...

POSEIDON. You have a talent for getting in trouble. Like your old man. *(He takes* **PERCY***'s backpack with the bolt.)* My brother will want his bolt back. Should've been the god of drama, that guy.

PERCY. I failed, Dad. The Oracle was right, I couldn't save what matters. I couldn't save Mom.

POSEIDON. You prevented a war between the gods! For that, well... the gods are unfair. But we're not total jerks.

PERCY. You mean she's...

POSEIDON. On her way now. *(A beat.)* Listen, before she gets here, there's something you should know. When summer ends, you can go home to her. Or you can stay at camp. Year-round.

PERCY. I didn't know I got a choice.

POSEIDON. Why do you think the gods stay out of their children's lives? The important choices are the ones you make for yourself. Still, I *am* sorry you were born.

PERCY. Wow, seriously?

POSEIDON. A hero's life is never easy.

[MUSIC NO. 14B – REUNITED]

*(**SALLY** enters, as **POSEIDON** disappears.)*

SALLY. Percy?

PERCY. Mom! You're alive!

SALLY. You saved me.

PERCY. And guess what, I met Dad, he's right over… *(Realizes.)* He's gone.

SALLY. That sounds like your dad.

PERCY. He told me about the choice I have to make. I can't leave you again, Mom.

SALLY. You saved my life. It's time I figure out how to live it.

PERCY. What are you going to do?

SALLY. I'll be like you. I'll be strong.

PERCY. I love you, Mom. *(**PERCY** hands **SALLY** the box.)* But if Gabe does give you any more trouble…

SALLY. "Care of Aunty Em's Garden Emporium?"

PERCY. It's a Do-It-Yourself Sculpture Kit. *(She starts to open it; he stops her.)* It's Medusa's head.

GROVER. So what now?

PERCY. *(To **GROVER**.)* As my Official Protector, you can officially escort us back to camp.

ANNABETH. And you're conscious this time!

[MUSIC NO. 15 – LAST DAY OF SUMMER]

(We transition to the trio arriving back at camp.)

PERCY. *(In his head.)*
WHAT DO YOU DO WHEN THE QUEST HAS ENDED?
WHAT DO YOU DO WHEN THE BATTLE'S WON?
SO MANY QUESTIONS LEFT UNANSWERED.
SO MANY THINGS STILL LEFT UNDONE.
AND WHAT DO YOU DO
WHEN IT'S UP TO YOU TO CHOOSE?
HAS SOMETHING ENDED OR BEGUN?
STAY OR GO?
PICK ONE.

*(As they enter camp, **CHIRON** greets them.)*

CHIRON. I hoofed it here as soon as I heard. All hail, Perseus Jackson, hero of Olympus!

*(Everyone cheers. But **PERCY** remains unsettled.)*

PERCY.
WHERE DO YOU GO
WHEN IT'S OVER?

PERCY & CAMPERS.
WHAT DO YOU DO
WHEN YOU'VE COME
TO THE LAST DAY OF SUMMER?

*(**PERCY** seeks out **LUKE** at the lake.)*

PERCY. Luke!

LUKE. If it isn't the big hero. Tough last day?

PERCY. I thought when I finished my quest, everything would make sense. But it doesn't. I never found out who stole the bolt for Ares, or what any of this has to do with Kronos. It's the last day of summer but I don't feel like anything's over.

LUKE. I get it.

CHIRON ALWAYS SAYS OUR PARENTS
MADE CAMP AS THIS "SAFE MAGIC SPACE."
THE TRUTH: IT'S SO THEY DON'T HAVE TO SEE US.
THEY WON'T BOTHER TO SHOW THEIR FACE!
IT'S TIME TO MAKE THE WORLD OUR OWN,
TIME SOMEONE PUT THEM IN THEIR PLACE!

Ares thought we were starting a war between the gods. But it was bigger than that. It was about wiping them out – and taking our turn.

PERCY. *(Realizes.)* You're the lightning thief.

(**PERCY** *draws his sword;* **LUKE** *draws his.*)

LUKE. The Oracle warned you. "Betrayed by a friend."

PERCY. You set me up. *You* told me to go to the Underworld. You were trying to free Kronos! *Why?*

LUKE. He's promised me the power to defeat our parents.

PERCY. He's using you! To get back at the gods!

LUKE. *Good!*

I'VE BEEN HERE SINCE I WAS A KID.
I DID EV'RYTHING THEY EVER ASKED,
YEAH, I DID.
AND FOR WHAT?

LUKE.	**CAMPERS.** *(Variously.)*
YOU KNOW THIS WORLD	
WILL NEVER BE OURS,	
AS LONG AS OUR PARENTS	WHAT DO YOU DO ON THE
RULE OVER THE STARS.	LAST DAY OF
SO I'LL DO ANYTHING	SUMMER? SUMMER,

LUKE.	**CAMPERS.** (*Variously.*)
I DON'T CARE IF I HURT ANYONE.	SUMMER, SUMMER, SUMMER, SUMMER
IT DOESN'T PAY TO BE A GOOD KID	SUMMER, SUMMER, SUMMER, SUMMER
A GOOD KID	SUMMER,
A GOOD SON.	SUMMER,
	SUMMER, SUMMER,
THE GODS ARE NEVER ON OUR SIDE,	SUMMER, SUMMER, SUMMER, SUMMER,
SO, I THINK IT'S TIME WE WATCH THEM FALL	SUMMER, SUMMER, SUMMER, SUMMER,
AND SOON YOU'LL SEE WHAT I DID	SUMMER, SUMMER, SUMMER, SUMMER,
SOON THERE'LL BE NO GODS AT ALL!	SUMMER, SUMMER, SUMMER, SUMMER, SUMMER, SUMMER,

(*By now, the whole camp has entered to hear this:* **ANNABETH, GROVER, CLARISSE,** *and* **CHIRON.**)

ANNABETH. Luke. What are you doing?

LUKE. What we promised. We said we'd never forget Thalia. (*To the Half-Bloods.*) Join me. We'll make the gods pay for what they did to her. To all of us.

PERCY. They've made mistakes! It doesn't mean we have to make them too.

LUKE. I know you'll choose wisely, Annabeth.

ANNABETH. You're right.

(**ANNABETH** *moves to* **LUKE***'s side – and disarms him.*)

It's over, Luke.

LUKE. It's not over yet. Well, it is for Percy.

> *(He pulls out a knife – fans know it's called*
> *Backbiter – and stabs* **PERCY** *in the shoulder.)*

PERCY. Ow!

ANNABETH. Percy!

> **(PERCY** *falls as* **LUKE** *flees.* **ANNABETH**
> *and the other campers gather around the*
> *unconscious* **PERCY**.*)*

CHIRON. *(To* **GROVER**, *re:* **LUKE**.*)* Go after him!

> **(GROVER** *runs after* **LUKE**.*)*

ANNABETH. Seaweed Brain?

> *(A beat. Finally* **PERCY** *opens his eyes.)*

PERCY. Wise girl?

> *(They move in close. Are they going to kiss?*
> *We never find out, because* **GROVER** *re-enters.)*

GROVER. He's gone.

ANNABETH. He'll be back.

CLARISSE. Then he'll be sorry.

CHIRON. This won't end with Luke. We stand on the brink of dangerous times. But if you choose to remain here, know that you'll have the full protection of the gods.

PERCY. No. Luke was right about one thing. We can't hide at camp waiting for our parents to fix things. We have to do it ourselves – out there, in the real world. That's where the monsters are.

ANNABETH. The gods will say we're impertinent.

PERCY. We *are* impertinent.

[MUSIC NO. 16 – BRING ON THE MONSTERS]

THERE'S GONNA BE A FIGHT.
THERE STILL MIGHT BE A WAR.
FOR THE MOMENT WE GOT
DANGER ON THE RUN.

ANNABETH.

AND THINGS'LL GET BAD,
BEFORE THEY WILL GET BETTER,
IT MAY FEEL LIKE AN ENDING
BUT THE BATTLE'S JUST BEGUN.

GROVER.

ARE WE EVER GONNA
ONCE HAVE IT EASY?

PERCY.

NOPE!
FEELIN' READY.

ANNABETH.

FEELIN' STOKED.

GROVER.

FEELIN' QUEASY.

ANNABETH.

WE COULD FAIL BUT WE HAVE TO TRY.

PERCY.

DON'T FEEL BAD,
'CAUSE WE'RE USUALLY ABOUT TO DIE!

PERCY, ANNABETH & GROVER.

BRING ON THE MONSTERS.
BRING ON THE MONSTERS.
BRING ON THE REAL WORLD.
BRING ON THE MONSTERS.

PERCY.

BRING ON THE REAL WORLD.

PERCY.	CHORUS.
BRING ON THE REAL WORLD.	AH
BRING ON THE REAL WORLD,	AH
THE REAL WORLD.	AH

PERCY.	ANNABETH.
AND I'LL BE BACK NEXT SUMMER,	BRING ON THE REAL WORLD.

PERCY.	GROVER.
YOU'LL SEE ME AGAIN,	DRIVE, JUST DRIVE.

PERCY.	GROVER.	ANNABETH.
I'LL BE BACK NEXT SUMMER	STAY AHEAD, AND STAY AHEAD	BRING ON THE REAL WORLD.

PERCY.	GROVER.
I'LL SURVIVE 'TIL THEN.	AND STAY ALIVE!

PERCY.

I'LL BE BACK NEXT SUMMER.

PERCY.	ANNABETH & CLARISSE.	CHIRON
YOU'LL SEE ME AGAIN.	BRING ON THE REAL WORLD.	NORMAL IS A MYTH.

PERCY.

I'LL BE BACK NEXT SUMMER.
I'LL BE BACK NEXT SUMMER.

PERCY.	ANNABETH.	CAMPERS.
I'LL BE BACK NEXT SUMMER,	BRING ON THE REAL WORLD.	WE'LL MAKE 'EM LISTEN TO US,

PERCY.		**CAMPERS.**
YOU'LL SEE ME AGAIN,		WE'LL MAKE 'EM LISTEN.

PERCY.	**ANNABETH.**	**CAMPERS.**
I'LL BE BACK NEXT SUMMER,	BRING ON ANY CHALLENGE.	WE'LL MAKE 'EM LISTEN TO US,

PERCY.		**CAMPERS.**
I'LL SURVIVE 'TIL THEN.		WE'LL MAKE 'EM LISTEN, OH.

PERCY.	**ANNABETH.**	**CAMPERS.**
AND I'LL BE BACK NEXT SUMMER,	BRING ON THE REAL WORLD.	WE'LL MAKE 'EM LISTEN TO US,

PERCY.		**CAMPERS.**
YOU'LL SEE ME AGAIN,		WE'LL MAKE 'EM LISTEN.

PERCY.
I'LL BE BACK NEXT SUMMER.
I'LL BE BACK NEXT SUMMER.

[MUSIC NO. 16A – BOWS/EXIT MUSIC]